HELEN'S SPECIAL CHRISTMAS

BY

PAT ATKINSON

Pat Atkinson
11-7-04

This book is a work of fiction. Places, events, and situations in this story are purely fictional. Any resemblance to actual persons, living or dead, is coincidental.

ISBN: 1-4033-4613-5 (e-book)
ISBN: 1-4033-4614-3 (Paperback)

Library of Congress Control Number: 2002092724

This book is printed on acid free paper.

Printed in the United States of America
Bloomington, IN

1st Books - rev. 11/06/02

THIS BOOK IS DEDICATED TO

My Mother, Helen Evelyn Keen Whitsett

She was a quiet, kind and gentle person with an inner strength, inherited from her ancestors. She was a good listener and patience was her greatest virtue. There was a little mischief lurking in back of those blue eyes from time to time but she was liked by everyone.

Edna Dee and James Keen taken in 1908

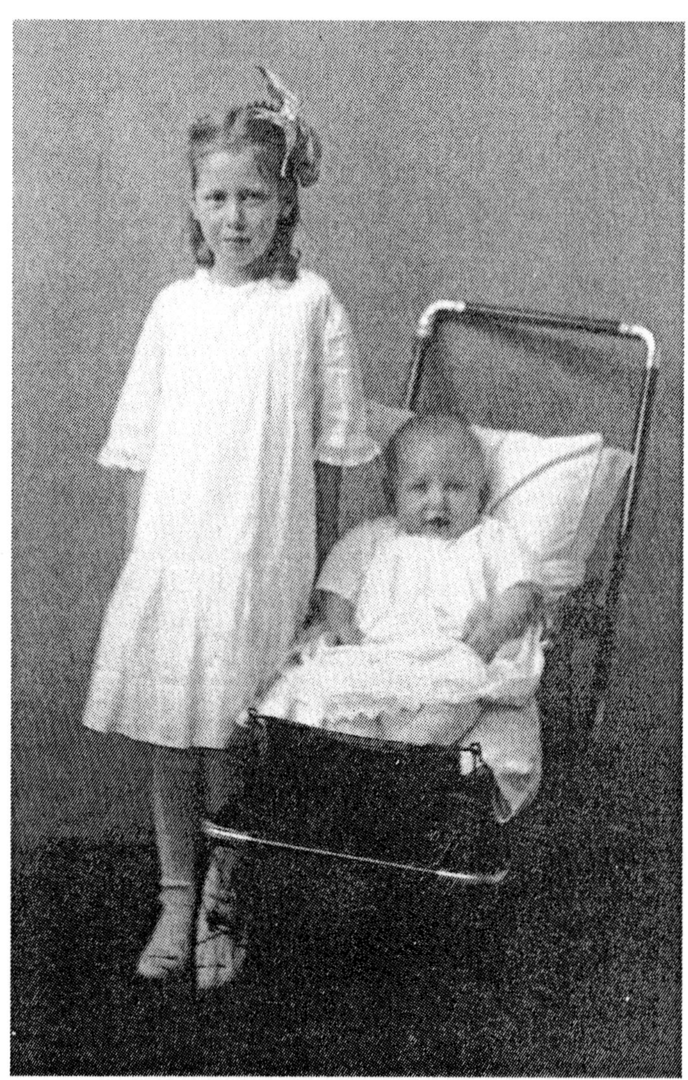

Helen and Kenneth Keen taken in 1915

This Christmas ...

We were gathered around the nearly perfect Christmas tree which glittered with more lights and ornaments than one could count. The roaring fire in the large fireplace, spread its cozy warmth through every inch of the room.

We had been joyfully singing carols to the music of Uncle Harold's guitar. Now the only sound was the crackling of the logs. A hush had fallen over us as we settled more comfortably into our seats.

It was time for Mother to once again reminisce about her special Christmas and the carved figures of Mary, Joseph and Baby Jesus in the manger. Every year they stood in their appointed place on a faded brown and green braided hot pad, next to an old, worn Bible with a tassle between the pages.

She began...

It was 1915 in a small Indiana town and "little" Helen Keen was six years old. Her relatives called her "little" Helen because she was named after Aunt Helen, her mother's sister.

Little Helen had a mother named Dee, a father named Jim, a baby brother named Kenny, many aunts and uncles and a special cousin named Carrie who was also her best friend. They did almost everything together.

Helen and Carrie had just finished tying string around some cornhusks to make new dolls. They had to do it very carefully so the head and body would be the right size.

It was nearly supper time and Helen needed to go home soon. Playing with the dolls would have to wait until tomorrow.

The girls knew that the next day would make it three weeks until Christmas. They had been counting the days since the month of December began.

Helen's and Carrie's Uncle Bert had a carpenter shop. Their fathers worked for him, making things from wood. Helen's father also worked with leather, making harnesses and sometimes repairing shoes and boots.

Carrie said her father was making her a sled for Christmas. Helen thought her father might make one for her too, but he liked to keep secrets so she wouldn't know about it until Christmas morning.

Helen could picture in her mind the new sleds and the two of them playing in the fluffy white snow, laughing and shouting with frost coming out of their mouths like puffs of smoke.

It was dark outside but Helen skipped home by the light of the street lamps. It was only one short block from Carrie's house to Helen's house so she was there in a jiffy.

She pushed open the kitchen door and found the kitchen was empty.

There was no fire in the cook stove and no smell of cooking food.

All of a sudden Helen's happy heart sank into her hungry stomach.

She knew something was wrong.

As she hurried through the kitchen, she heard muffled voices coming from the sitting room. It was Dr. Strong, talking to her mother, who was standing with Kenny in her arms. Helen's father was sitting on the edge of the chair, looking tired and scared. Helen's mother turned toward her. She had tears in her eyes and on her face.

One of the doctor's hands was on her mother's arm and the other one on her father's shoulder. He was saying, "Now Dee, we need to wait and see what happens. It could go away as fast as it came. Jim, you just relax and try to get some rest. I'll come back tomorrow and see if there is any change. If you need me, just send Helen."

He nodded seriously and quietly let himself out through the seldom used front door.

Helen stood still, waiting for her mother to explain what had happened. Fear was there in her stomach too, making her feel sick.

After a long minute, it was her father who explained. He sat still as if in a daze. He didn't move his body and hardly opened his mouth. His voice was shaky and low. "Helen, sweetheart, something has happened to your daddy; he can't move his hand."

Helen was afraid to look at his hand because she knew that actually seeing it would make it true.

Finally she dared to glance down. Her father's limp right hand was lying on the arm of the chair. Sudden tears clouded Helen's eyes until she couldn't see the hand at all.

Her father, always so strong and capable of anything, sat fearful and helpless there before her. What could she do? She ran and flung herself onto her bed and sobbed. She eventually fell asleep with her coat and dress on and no supper in her empty stomach.

Helen awoke to the shrill whistle of the seven o'clock train which passed near their house every morning. She should be getting ready for school. What day was it and why was she wearing her coat and dress? Then she remembered her father. Her troubled mind tried to recall the details of the night before. She listened but heard no one stirring.

Helen silently crept to the bedroom door and looked through the sitting room to the kitchen. No one was there. She shivered in the cold of the December morning. It was dark and no fire was burning in the stove. Helen crept back to bed and pulled the quilt over her head. It seemed like she was all alone and even though her bed was warm, she shivered again.

In Sunday School, Miss Penny had said we are never alone. God watches over us all the time. Was God watching now? How could God watch over everyone in the whole world at the same time, especially when it is dark? Helen would ask Miss Penny the next time she told them a Bible story about God watching over someone.

Miss Penny had also said God always hears us. She said that when we pray and talk to God, He hears everything we say. Helen tried to understand how He could do that. Heaven was so far away and if everyone was talking at the same time, how could God sort out who was saying what? Helen knew what it was like when all of the relatives were together at Thanksgiving. Everyone would be trying to tell things at the same time and it was so noisy with the babies crying and all, that no one could understand anything.

When Helen opened her eyes again, the sun was shining. She heard Kenny crying and her mother's voice. Maybe everything was back to normal. The cheerful sun streaming through the windows and the stove giving off warmth gave Helen enough hope to spring out of bed and run to the door. But she stopped there as she saw her father sitting at the table, eating his breakfast with his left hand.

Nothing had changed.

Helen's mother turned from the stove and saw her standing in the doorway. "Go on to the outhouse and then wash your hands and face for breakfast. The day's half gone."

She looked stern so Helen ran outside as soon as she put on her shoes.

It was cold in the outhouse even though the sun was shining and it was chilly inside Helen's heart as well.

Breakfast was on the table as soon as Helen came back inside.

It was mush, as usual, with some of the cream from "Old Rose" their mostly brown cow.

She sat down and looked sadly at her father. He held his finger to his mouth, which meant she should not say anything. So she sat with downcast eyes and wished she could eat faster.

Helen's mother hurried around the kitchen, pretending to be busy. As Helen finished, her mother came and stood beside her and said, "Now Helen, since your father is laid up with his hand, I will have to do some of his chores and you will have to help out with some of my chores. I need you to be a good girl and do as you are told without talking back. Will you try to be a good helper?"

Helen nodded, looking at the cracks in the floor. Her father chimed in, trying to sound cheerful. "Sure she will, Dee. I'll be as good as new before long and then she can go back to her dolls."

With all her heart, Helen hoped he was right.

Later that day, after she had swept the floors, helped wash the dishes and helped make the beds, her mother said she could go to Carrie's house and play for a while.

Helen had forgotten about the new corn husk dolls they had made the day before. She put on her coat and hat and slowly walked to Carrie's house, as small snow flakes floated down from the sky. The sun was gone now and everything looked gray and dreary.

Carrie saw Helen from the window and came to open the door. She started chattering about the dolls.

Helen really didn't want to play. Her heart just wasn't in it today. Her whole life had changed since yesterday; didn't Carrie know that!

Then Carrie said some terrible things. She said, "You know, Helen, now that your father can't work anymore, Uncle Bert had to hire someone else to help him. With only three weeks 'til Christmas, he will be very busy. You won't be getting your sled either but you can slide on mine if you want to."

Helen just looked at her in amazement. Aunt Flo, Carrie's mother, walked over and said sternly, "Hush Carrie, how you blabber. You're hurting Helen's feelings."

Helen wanted to cry. She didn't care about the sled, really, but she never thought about her Daddy not being able to work anymore. Carrie was wrong. Helen knew her Daddy would get better soon. She just knew it!

Aunt Flo was making corn bread and the girls sat down at the table to have some, with milk. It tasted like grit in Helen's mouth. No matter what anyone said or did now, it was too late to take it back. Helen wanted to go home and as soon as she choked down her corn bread, that is what she did.

When Helen walked through the kitchen door, her father was putting coal into the stove as best he could with one hand. Helen hurried over to help him.

He was surprised to see her back home so soon. “Didn’t Carrie want to play?” he asked.

“It was I who didn’t want to play, Daddy; and besides, Carrie said a terrible thing.”

He turned his full attention to Helen then. “What did she say?”

“She said you can’t work and Uncle Bert had to hire someone else to help him. Who will work so we can buy things, Daddy?”

Jim tried to sound sure of himself when he answered. "I will work but it will have to be at something different. We will see what happens in a few days. We can pray and God will tell us what to do. In the meantime, you mind your mother and help as much as you can. Will you do that?" He patted her on the shoulder and she felt better already.

"I promise," she said.

"It will be simple food from now on Helen, and no complaining," said her mother, at the supper table.

Helen made a face at the kraut and dumplings in front of her. The side meat could hardly be seen. The rule in that house had always been that you cleaned up your plate or you found the same food on it at the next meal. Helen knew cold kraut and dumplings wouldn't taste very good for breakfast the next day.

That night, while Helen's mother was taking care of Kenny, her father came to tuck her into bed. They had already let the fire in the stove go out and only one oil lamp burned low in the sitting room.

As Jim's tall body came through the doorway, he looked like his old self in the almost darkness. He sat down on Helen's bed and turned toward her.

Helen summoned up all the courage she had and in that moment's time she blurted out, "Daddy, let me hold your poor, lame hand while we say our prayer."

Helen quickly put her soft, little hand into Jim's big palm. She knew he couldn't feel her hand but he knew it was there. Then she said so quietly that he could hardly hear her, "Dear Heavenly Father, please heal my Daddy's poor, weak hand and help me to be a good helper. In Jesus' name, amen."

Quickly she took her hand away. Her father did not speak. He only pulled the handmade quilt up to Helen's chin and patted her cheek as he turned and left the room.

Helen knew in her heart that God had heard her prayer. She just knew He would heal her Daddy's hand.

Sunday was always a day for family gatherings. Everyone got up early on Sunday to get ready for church and then they would hurry home to fix dinner for the company who came. With such a large family, there was always company on Sunday.

This Sunday it would be Helen's cousin Elizabeth from about fifteen miles away in another town. Elizabeth's father would be bringing some meat he had cured in his smokehouse. In her mind, Helen could taste it already.

In Sunday School, Miss Penny had the children practice their parts for the Christmas play which would be in two weeks. Helen was an angel and the whole group of angels would recite the Bible verses about the Heavenly Host speaking to the shepherds. They would also sing “Joy To The World” all by themselves. Everyone was excited.

Helen skipped all the way home from church. She didn’t even walk with Carrie like she usually did.

When Helen got home, everyone was already there, including her Uncle Ed and three year old Elizabeth. Elizabeth's mother stayed home because she was going to have a baby very soon – maybe even on Christmas Day! Uncle Ed and Elizabeth didn't stay for dinner because Ed wanted to get back.

As they were leaving, Elizabeth stood up in the wagon and announced in a loud voice, "My baby brother will be Baby Jesus in our play at school, so there."

Her father sat her down on the wooden seat with a bang. “He will be no such thing, you silly girl. Don’t speak so foolish’. Now say ‘goodbye’.”

Elizabeth just sat and pouted. Uncle Ed waved and the two horses lurched ahead as he gave them the reins. Off they went, into the distance.

"Maybe Kenny could be Baby Jesus in our play," Helen said with eyes wide. She had never thought of that. They were using a rolled up cloth for their Baby Jesus. Her mother looked sideways at her and she knew better than to say more. On second thought, he might cry at the wrong time and spoil everything.

That night, it worked out that Helen's father came to tuck her in again; only this time it was earlier because she had to get up for school in the morning.

Helen was more brave about his hand and while she prayed for it, she touched each one of his fingers. She certainly hoped Miss Penny was right about God hearing everything. She was pretty sure last night but a whole day had gone by and that hand was still the same.

The next morning when the seven o'clock train came whistling through town, Helen was washing her face and hands for breakfast. It was snowing outside and she thought again about the sled she would not be getting for Christmas. She didn't care, she said to herself. She just wanted her daddy's hand to get better, that's all.

Helen loved school. They had a nice, new schoolhouse three blocks away and she loved her teacher, Miss Dial. Everyone loved Miss Dial because she was so kind. She wouldn't let the big boys pick on the smaller children. Also as each child passed through the schoolhouse door, Miss Dial was there to give them a hug. Some of the children pretended they didn't like it but Helen knew that deep down, they did.

As it was getting closer to Christmas, Miss Dial let the children spend a little time each day, making paper chains to decorate the room. They made red and green ones and some were neat and some were messy but all of them were used. She also showed them how to make little paper angels that could stand up alone. They would take their angels home on the last day of school before Christmas.

The days passed by slowly. Helen's father did what he could, considering his lame hand. He couldn't milk "Old Rose" the cow, but every day when the trains went through town, he could take a gunny sack to the tracks and pick up lumps of coal which had fallen off the coal cars.

He picked up sticks to light the fires, he carried water from the pump and always right by his side would be his faithful dog, "Wolf". Wolf had his own dog house out by the back fence but he could be found near the kitchen door most of the time. Helen's mother said he was always underfoot and would grumble about him, but she had to admit he was a good watchdog.

Jim often told about the time the band of gypsies came to town and Wolf barked and howled 'til all those gypsies ran away.

Every night, Helen would pray out loud for her daddy and his poor, lame hand. Every night she. would hold that hand and stroke it lovingly, asking her daddy if he could feel anything. Every night he said he could feel a little more.

Their meals these days were mostly potato soup, bread and jam, bread and milk, soup beans and bread or bread and butter if Helen's mother had churned the cream from "Old Rose". Then there was always mush or hominy grits for breakfast. The meat Uncle Ed had brought would be saved for Sunday dinners and especially for Christmas dinner.

Helen tried to be happy even though she knew Christmas would be a lean one at their house this year. Carrie bragged that she was making gifts for her mother and father but she was keeping them a secret. Helen wished she could make something too. Then she had an idea.

Helen asked Miss Dial if she would show her how to make some simple gifts because this year she wouldn't have money to buy anything. The teacher thought about it and came up with an idea of her own. Miss Dial announced to the class that any boy or girl who had permission and wanted to make a simple gift, could stay after school each day and she would help them.

Miss Dial would make sample gifts for the children to choose from and use as a guide to make their own.

Helen was excited. Now she would have a secret just like Carrie and she would also have gifts for her mother and daddy. She wondered what ideas Miss Dial had for simple gifts that children could make. She tried to picture some things in her mind but they were all too difficult, so she gave up thinking about it.

Miss Dial would tell them her plans on Monday and Helen could hardly wait. She was so bubbly around the house that her mother wondered what had gotten into her. Because of this, she sat down and called Helen to her side. She must be sure Helen wasn't expecting too much for Christmas.

Dee told Helen sadly that there would be very little that year. They must remember the real meaning of Christmas was to celebrate the birth of Jesus Christ, God's Son. God's Gift was the most important one, not what we give to each other.

Helen said, "Yes, Mother, I won't be disappointed." She hoped it was true.

Helen's father could move his hand now and feel things. Helen was sure God was answering her nightly prayers. He still couldn't work but he could do more chores and that meant she would be able to stay after school to make gifts. She dared not think about not being able to stay after school since the whole thing was her idea. Well, at least the beginning part was.

On Monday, Miss Dial asked who wanted to stay. Twelve children raised their hands. She put some things on her desk for them to choose. They were things she had made as samples. Helen chose a hot pad for her mother and a book mark for her daddy. Miss Dial said she would have to bring some rags and string to school the next day and a note from her mother saying she had permission to stay a half hour after school each day until her gifts were finished.

There were only eight days until school let out for the holidays. They would have to hurry with their projects.

Helen ran all the way home from school and was out of breath as she burst through the kitchen door. She bounced around the room until her mother said, "Sit down girl, you're shaking the house."

"Oh Mother," she said between gasps, "Miss Dial is showing us how to make some things for gifts. It was my idea and some of the others want to do it too and I need to take a note saying I can and some rags and string to school tomorrow. We have to hurry because there are only eight more days."

"Slow down Missy, this is the first I've heard of such a thing. What was your idea?" So Helen slowly told her mother the whole story, hoping she would agree to let her do it.

At the end, Dee said, "What can you children make from rags and string, I'd like to know."

"It's a secret, but Miss Dial made samples and we got to choose. May I, Mother? Please say 'yes'."

Her mother looked doubtful. Finally she said, "I'll see if I can find some rags and string and if I can, I will write a note."

That night when Helen said her prayers about her daddy's hand, she also had to pray that her mother would find some rags and string. Right now, everything depended on it. She could always ask her many aunts if they had some but her mother would never allow it. She could just hear her mother saying, "Imagine asking people to give you rags and string. What in the world are you thinking about, girl?"

Helen had a dream about making beautiful gifts for everyone and when the seven o'clock train whistled through town, she was ready for school.

Dee was able to find some rags and string and Helen had her note tucked safely in the bottom of her coat pocket.

God had heard and answered her prayer.

The childen could hardly wait to start their gifts. Miss Dial told them not to rush and to do a good job. She helped Helen pull a thread to see where she should tear her cloth into strips so they would be straight and even. Then she showed her how to braid the strips into long braids. It was just like braiding hair only it had to be very tight.

Since it was later when Helen was walking home from school now, the houses along the way had their lamps lit for the evening. She could look into the kitchens and sitting rooms. She could see the mothers cooking supper and children playing. It looked so cheerful and warm inside, Helen thought to herself as she walked slowly past.

"These people are all happy in their cozy houses with their fires stoked up and their suppers of meat and potatoes and gravy and apple pie," she said to herself, out loud. She knew she was feeling sorry for herself. She was cold and hungry.

Then she heard someone calling her name. She turned around and saw that it was Joe, coming toward her.

Joe was a raggedy eight year old boy from down the street. He had something wrong with his leg and he couldn't walk very well. His little sister, Nell, had died last summer from a bad disease. No one could go in or out of their house.

It was so hot outside on the day of Nell's funeral and people were afraid to go. Helen's Uncle Bert had made a little casket and just gave it to the family because they were so poor.

Helen felt sorry for Joe but at the same time, she was afraid.

"Are ya makin' gifts at school?" he asked.

"Yes," she answered. "Are you?"

"Naw, my ma said we got no stuff ta make 'em with, so I ain't. You got stuff?"

"Yes," said Helen. "Rags and string."

"Don't got no rags ner string ner wood ner nowheres ta git 'em from neither." He hobbled along beside Helen.

Helen thought about wood and she knew there might be some scraps in Uncle Bert's shop. She could ask about it for Joe. Better not tell him yet, though, and get his hopes up.

Helen turned into her yard and Joe went on alone, slowly and sadly hobbling along, looking at the ground.

She watched as he opened the door to his own house where no light shown through the window and she was sure no meat and potatoes and gravy would be on the supper table there either.

She had to ask her daddy about the wood scraps as soon as she could.

By the weekend, Helen had her strips all torn evenly and some of them braided. She had to finish braiding and get them sewn together in four days, plus make the string bookmark. For once, she wished there were more days of school before Christmas.

On Saturday, Helen went to the church to practice the Christmas play. They would do everything just like it would be done on Sunday. There were so many things to remember. She had heard that her cousin Elizabeth now had a baby brother. She thought about him when Mary put Baby Jesus into the manger during the play.

Their Baby Jesus was just a rolled up cloth. Miss Penny said that way no one had to worry about dropping a real baby by mistake or having him cry during the play. There was no way to guess when a baby might decide to cry. She knew that because of Kenny.

Carrie was an angel also but she had a real angel dress. Aunt Flo had made it especially for the play. Helen just had her regular church dress and so did all the other angels.

Helen's mother could have made her a special angel dress if she hadn't been so busy with Kenny and doing the milking and everything else. Right at that moment, Helen gave a brief thought to the fact that she probably could have helped her mother around the house, a little more often lately.

That evening it began to snow and all night great big, wet flakes chased each other down from the sky. When Helen got up the next morning, she had to put on her boots to get to the out-house.

The whole town was covered in white. It looked like a giant Christmas card. Aunt June had sent them one last year from New York and it was beautiful but a real live Christmas card like this was much better. There were some times when one could be very quiet and hear the snow fall. This morning was one of those times. Helen breathed in the cold air and listened to the snow. It was wonderful but would soon be spoiled by barking dogs and people getting out and about, their boots making a path of footprints as they crunch, crunch, crunched to town.

The program was to be at 4:00 in the afternoon. All the families would come from the farms and from town. There would be wagons and sleighs from the country and all the horses would be tied to the hitching posts.

Helen loved to see the horses. She liked the dark brown ones best. Some of the horses had sleigh bells on their harnesses. Some of those harnesses had even been made by her daddy.

Helen also loved to hear the sleigh bells jingling in the crisp, clear night air, long after the sleigh was out of sight. At the same time, it gave her a sort of hollow, lonely feeling like someone was leaving her forever. She guessed it was something like the feeling her mother had when she heard a train whistle in the distance. "A lonesome feeling," she said.

But there was no time for looking at horses or feeling lonesome today because Helen had to be in place at the very beginning of the program to sing "Silent Night" with the other angels and the shepherds. Miss Penny wanted everything to be just right. She said God would be watching. Helen didn't have a chance to ask about God seeing us all the time because Miss Penny was too busy.

During the program, Helen dared to look through the audience to find out who had come especially to see her perform. There was Aunt Helen and Aunt Marie. She was sure Aunt Bess and Aunt June would have come if it hadn't been for the snow. They lived so far away and Helen hardly ever got to see them.

Aunt Susie just had the baby and Aunt Ruth was working away from home. Aunts Linnie and Libby and Clara were there, of course, because they lived in town.

At the end of the program, every child received a stick of peppermint candy. It had red and white stripes and many of the children had red and sticky faces and hands before they ever arrived back home that night. Helen saved hers to enjoy a little at a time.

The excited children were having snowball fights and running up and down the usually quiet streets. The moon was so bright as it came out of the east that Helen thought it almost looked like morning.

In the store one time, she had seen a Christmas card with a big moon on it and a little church. There was a little house too, with candles in the windows. She could imagine the people who lived in that house, gathered around the fireplace on Christmas Eve, reading the Christmas story from the Bible. There would be a mother and father and children all nestled there in a haven of warmth.

Helen knew she was a dreamer. She liked to imagine things in her mind. Sometimes they seemed almost real.

As they came inside and shook the snow off their coats, Helen's mother put the kettle on for tea. She looked sad. Helen was sorry, in a way, that the play was over. It seemed like Christmas was over too. Well, she still had the stick of candy anyway.

When her mother saw her looking at the candy, she said "Better save that for Christmas; it may be all you'll get."

In the last four days of school, Helen finished braiding her rags and sewed them together in a circle to make the hot pad for her mother. It was faded brown and green from an old dress Dee used to wear.

She had also carefully braided lengths of string to make a bookmark with a tassle on the end, for her daddy. She was happy with her gifts and grateful to Miss Dial, their wonderful teacher.

As the children left the schoolhouse the day before Christmas Eve, Helen had her gifts deep in her coat pocket and her paper angel in her hand.

Some of the children were playing in the snow on their way home but Helen hurried along. She did not want to lose anything or have her angel ruined by a snowball.

She was almost to her yard when someone yelled, "Wait up, wait up." She didn't want to look back, but she did. It was Joe.

"Hey Helen, wait up 'n' look at the gifts I made with the wood scraps ya found." He was waving a long stick back and forth between them.

"What's that?" Helen asked, laughing.

"It's fer my pa ta measure stuff with. Miss Dial helped me mark it off fer inches. It's twelve inches long. Now my pa c'n measure stuff anytime he needs ta."

"Did you make anything else?" Helen asked.

He pulled his crumpled paper angel out of his pocket and a small cross made of two pieces of wood nailed together and then nailed to a flat piece of wood, so it would stand alone.

"This is fer my ma ta put on the table where she prays," he said as he held it in the air and admired it. "This here was my own idea," he bragged, pointing to himself with his thumb.

Helen admired it too. "That was a nice idea, Joe. I'm sure your mother will like it."

Helen started to turn away. She didn't want to show her gifts to Joe so she didn't want to give him the chance to ask.

He was stuffing the cross and angel back into his pocket. It wasn't polite to walk away but Joe was just standing there.

"I hope you have a nice Christmas," Helen said hesitantly, thinking of his sister dying and all.

Joe finally summoned the courage to ask, "Do ya have a Christmas tree?"

Helen wondered why he asked. "No, do you?" She was glad she didn't have one, just incase he didn't.

He shook his head. "My pa said it's too sad ta have Christmas 'cause a Nell 'n' we got no gifts, but now I got gifts 'n' I'm gonna find a tree anyway."

"Where?" she asked.

"Don' know but if I find one, I'll come 'n' tell ya." He nodded to make it more of a sure thing.

"How will you cut it down?"

"Don' know. I'll see when I get there. Gotta go." He hobbled away through the deep snow, leaving Helen to wonder what he was really talking about.

Helen shrugged and pushed her gifts more firmly into her pocket, as she entered the house, just to be sure they would not be seen.

She hadn't really thought about a Christmas tree. She had gifts now too and up until today her mind had been taken up with them.

Where would she put her gifts if they didn't have a tree?

Tomorrow was only Christmas Eve so there was still time.

The next morning when Helen awoke, she realized that it was indeed Christmas Eve. They would certainly have a white Christmas.

She could hear sleigh bells and laughter as people from the country were coming to town for food and gifts. Everyone had the Christmas spirit of good will toward men.

"Wolf" barked and jumped excitedly at everything.

After breakfast, Helen went outside to make a snowman. It would be her first one of the year. This snow was easy to pack and make into big balls. She was so busy rolling those balls that when she turned around, there stood Joe.

She jumped in surprise. "Where did you come from?" she asked.

"I'll show ya where ya c'n get a tree," he said.

"Where?"

"Come on with me down ta the ol' shack."

Helen frowned. "What would a Christmas tree be doing at the old shack?" She knew it had been abandoned a long time ago but there still was a big, tall pine tree in the front yard. It reached far up into the sky.

"You'll see," he said as he started to leave.

"Wait Joe, I can't just go without permission and how can we cut it down?"

"Don' need ta cut it down – you'll see, come on." He was getting impatient. He was hobbling away and then he turned around and said, "Come on" again, urgently.

Helen looked toward the house and then hurried to catch up with Joe, who somehow seemed to be going faster and faster.

The old shack was past Joe's house, on the edge of town. It was an empty, weatherbeaten and forsaken place and also kind of scarey.

When they arrived there, Joe went around back to where the outhouse was and part of an old woodshed. "What would a Christmas tree be doing here?" Helen asked herself.

Helen stopped and let Joe go on, climbing through snow drifts and sometimes almost losing his balance. He forged ahead, not bothering to see if Helen was following.

Helen knew there were unknown things under the pure white snow that she didn't want to know about. She didn't like it here at all and was about to turn away when Joe yelled.

"Come on, Helen, get over here 'n' pick it out." He beckoned to her from the window of the woodshed. She really didn't want to "get over there" but Joe would think she was a scaredy cat. She hesitated and then tried to follow Joe's waggly trail, carefully creeping through the knee deep sea of white.

Banked up against a half wall, sheltered by a sort of lean-to, were many brown tumbleweeds as big as a small Christmas tree. They had blown in there from the fields right outside the door, before the deep snow had fallen.

Joe held up one and gleefully yelled, "This un's mine – git yers."

"What kind of a Christmas tree is that?" Helen snickered.

"One that don' need cuttin' down. I figure on findin' some ol' jar ta sit it in 'n' put the paper angel on top. Hey, it's better'n nothin'."

Helen had to agree. The idea of the angel on top was a good one. No one at her house had said anything about a tree. Her daddy could not cut down a tree this year and a tumbleweed tree would be better than none at all.

She hurriedly picked one and they worked their way back to the street. Helen breathed a sigh of relief.

As they came to Joe's house, he said in a low voice behind his hand, as if someone was eavesdropping, "I only told ya about the tumbleweeds 'cause ya got wood scraps fer me. I knew ya wouldn' make fun a me like the others do."

He turned and hobbled toward his little home with his tumbleweed Christmas tree proudly held high.

Helen watched with tears in her eyes. They both would have tumbleweed Christmas trees. She knew Carrie would make fun of it but she didn't care. Maybe Joe would be her best friend from now on.

Helen carried the tumbleweed carefully into the house and looked up to see her mother's unhappy face. It was what she had feared. Her mother knew she had left the yard without permission and on Christmas Eve of all days.

She knew no explanation would be good enough, but she said it anyway. "I had to go with Joe to get this Christmas tree. He was leaving without me. We only went to the old shack."

Dee stood with her hands on her hips. "Christmas tree, my foot; that's a tumbleweed as sure as I'm standing here. You know better than to go off without permision, especially with the likes of Joe. Young lady, you go stand in the corner 'til your father gets back from picking up coal – something you could have done if you'd been here. Christmas Eve and so much to do and you lollygagging around town with Joe." She sounded disgusted.

Helen carried her tumbleweed along to the corner of the kitchen. She knew her mother was disappointed in her. It was too late now, the deed was done. The tumbleweed idea sounded good a little while ago but now she would be punished and all she had to show for it was this old, brown wisp of a thing she still held tightly in her hand. She was even disappointed in herself.

The door opened, letting in the cold air and some stray snowflakes. Helen's father stomped in, carrying the coal scuttle. At first, he didn't see Helen in the corner and sat down to take off his boots.

Jim looked up and saw that his wife was upset. "What's wrong?" he asked.

Dee started right in with her side of the story. "Helen left the yard without permission – said she went to the old shack with Joe and came home with a tumbleweed which she says is a Christmas tree. Now Jim, you make sense of that!"

Jim looked at Helen and burst out laughing. It was the most he had laughed since his hand went limp. Helen was indeed a pityful sight, standing in the corner, holding a tumbleweed.

Then his wife continued, "Christmas Eve and so much to do. Helen out lollygagging around town..."

Helen knew her father had to get serious because her mother was very serious.

They were both surprised when Jim said, "Christmas Eve is no day for standing in the corner. I say we trim that Christmas tree."

Dee shook her head and said, "Well, I never know what's on your mind, Jim Keen!"

Helen bounced over to her father. "Daddy, I'm so glad you like my tree. What can we trim it with? I have my paper angel for the top."

Jim had a twinkle in his eye as he pretended to think. "I'd say we need to string some berries and some popcorn." Then he looked at his wife and said, "Don't worry so much about the chores. We've got a tree to trim and we need your help."

Helen and her daddy went to pick Holly berries for stringing and Helen's mother popped a little corn for stringing too.

Helen hoped Joe had something to decorate his tree with besides that crumpled paper angel from school. Then she smiled and said to herself, "Knowing Joe, he probably has the best decorated tumbleweed in town."

The three of them had fun decorating the tree which was now standing in a jug Helen's father found in the woodshed. The angel was at the very top and the berries and popcorn were wrapped around and around.

After Christmas they would put the tree outside and the birds could have a little food to eat without searching for it in the deep snow. Helen felt good about that.

Everything was working out after all.

Helen dared to hang her stocking up on a nail in the sitting room, as she did every Christmas Eve. She hoped there might be an apple or orange in it the next morning as there always had been on Christmas morning. She remembered though, that her mother had warned her about expecting too much; that there might not be a gift so she must not be disappointed if there was nothing.

Besides, God's Gift of His Son was the most important gift. Her father always read about the first Christmas and the birth of God's Son from his worn Bible, on Christmas morning. Helen almost knew it by heart.

Helen's plan was to get out of bed as soon as the house was dark and put the bookmark in her daddy's Bible. That way, when he opened it to read the story in the morning, he would be surprised. She would put her mother's hot pad under the tree and go quietly back to bed.

It would not be easy to find everything in the dark, though, and after she was tucked into her warm bed and the lamp was snuffed out, she changed her mind. She decided to get up early in the morning and do everything.

The seven o'clock train whistled through town even on Christmas Day and that is what woke Helen from her dreams. All of a sudden she realized that her gifts were still right there in bed with her and not under the tree. What could she do?

She heard voices in the kitchen and smelled cooking food. The lamp was lit and the wood fire crackled.

She had slept too long.

She quietly took the gifts and set them under the tree. There was no time to do anything else. She was afraid to, but she couldn't keep from looking at her stocking which was still hanging on the nearby nail. It was empty.

Right then she wanted to cry and tried to swallow the lump in her throat, when something came to mind that the old preacher had once said. "It is more blessed to give than to receive."

She stood, her bare feet on the cold floor, for a long time, wondering what could have happened. The limp stocking was as empty as could be. She was sure not even a tiny gift was inside.

She was still standing there when Jim came through the doorway from the kitchen. He held something in his hand and her mother was right behind him. That was strange. Was something wrong?

Jim walked over to Helen and gave her what he was holding. It was wrapped in brown paper.

"Sit down, sweetheart, and open your gift; but be careful not to drop anything."

Helen was more surprised than she had ever been on Christmas morning. Usually there was an apple or an orange and maybe a stick of candy in her stocking and this year she had guessed there might be a sled if her daddy had been working for Uncle Bert.

But there was no sled and even her stocking was empty. What could this be in the brown paper? She could not even imagine.

As Helen carefully opened the paper, she discovered three carved figures. One was Mary, one was Joseph and one was Baby Jesus in the manger. They were made of lovely, dark wood and they were so smooth to touch.

Helen looked up in disbelief.

"Daddy, how could you make these with your crippled hand?"

Jim knelt beside her and lifted each piece he had so lovingly carved. "It is because of your prayers that God healed my hand and while God was healing my hand, I was able to carve this Holy Family for my favorite daughter. The carving helped my hand get strong again and soon I will be able to go back to work and finish your Christmas sled."

"Oh, the Holy Family and a sled too!" Helen wrapped her arms around her daddy's neck. "This is the best Christmas ever."

"I want to put the family in a special place under the Christmas tree," Helen said, as she turned toward it. Then she remembered the gifts she had placed there earlier.

Helen presented her mother with the hot pad and her daddy with the bookmark. They were so pleased that their daughter had thought more about giving than receiving.

Jim opened his Bible to the second chapter of Luke and put the bookmark there. Dee took the hot pad to the kitchen and used it to lift the kettle from the cookstove. She had to admit something useful could be made by the school children from rags and string.

After their breakfast of mush and some of Uncle Ed's bacon, they went to the sitting room where Jim opened his Bible to the book of Luke and prepared to read.

Helen summoned up the courage, just as she had done once before, and asked, "Daddy, may I hold your hand, just to make sure it is strong again?"

"You most certainly may," he said as he grabbed her hand and squeezed it.

Helen knew the verses from Luke because of the Christmas program at church. The angels had even recited some of them. She tried to imagine what it had been like when Jesus was born in the stable in Bethlehem. Now she had her carved family to help her picture it.

When Jim finished reading, Helen asked if she could say a thank you prayer.

They bowed their heads and in a quiet voice, Helen said, "Dear Heavenly Father, thank You for sending Your Son down to earth, thank You for making my daddy's hand strong again, thank You that You are always watching over us, even when it is dark; thank You that You always hear us even when everyone is talking at once; thank You for my mother and daddy and for Kenny and my friend Joe." She stopped to be sure she hadn't forgotten anything and realized that she had... "And now that everything is right again, please help me to forgive Carrie for the terrible thing she said that day. In Jesus' name, amen."

A sense of God's presence flowed through the room. Then a voice near the fireplace broke the silence by asking, "Mother, did you, I mean, did Little Helen ever forgive Carrie?"

"Of course," she replied, "but that's a story for another time."

ACKNOWLEDGMENTS

To any creative person, their creation becomes like their child; the world should recognize how wonderful it is. Thankfully there are friends with unbiased opinions (hopefully) who will spot any blemishes before the world has a chance to see them and bring the creator back to reality. Here is my list of such friends and relatives:

Breanne Alexander, Robert J. Atkinson, Richard Blair, Marjorie Bonham, Sandra Bublis, Jami Dean, Sister Mary Dolores Greifer, Enos and Linda Howard, Mark and Belinda Kaminski, Isabella Banks Adams Keen, Jeanne Dee Keen, Susan Lucas, Nancy McIntire, Eileen Murray, Pastor Leon Pomeroy and Robert A. Waitches.

Additionally I would like to thank Marj Bonham for being my advisor, counselor and shepherd; Sandy Bublis for all the opportunities she has given me; Eileen Murray who prods me on with her enthusiastic "can do" attitude and Bob Waitches whom I can always count on for constructive suggestions and support.

Thanks to my good friend Robert E. Calvert. In the old days Bob and I inspired each other over countless cups of coffee at "The Family Tree". There was a sort of magic in those conversations. " No other person has come close to being the creative inspiration you have been to me through the years."

A special thanks to the late Charles W. Austin and his wife Leora who did exhaustive research on the Joseph Prosper Austin side of the family and included us in their book on the Austin Family. " Without you, we would have very little reference material. We are very grateful for it."

And thanks be to God who gives us everything and without Him we would be nothing. I pray that He will put this book into all the right hands and hearts and bless each one.

ABOUT THE AUTHOR

I have loved to write all my life. In fact, I was writing (making very small marks with a pencil, on everything) before I could walk or talk. My main interest is fiction, focusing on people and the way they act and think. *Helen's Special Christmas* is my second book to be published, the first one being entitled *Winning is Your Choice: A Guide to Salvation.* I hope to retire soon and devote more time to writing.

Printed in the United States
773900001B